Gypsy In The Hills

Musharaf Fayaz

 pencil

ISBN 978-93-5667-022-8
© Musharaf Fayaz 2022
Published in India 2022 by Pencil

Contributors:
Co-Author: Abeer Bin Javid

A brand of
One Point Six Technologies Pvt. Ltd.
123, Building J2, Shram Seva Premises,
Wadala Truck Terminal, Wadala (E)
Mumbai 400037, Maharashtra, INDIA
E connect@thepencilapp.com
W www.thepencilapp.com

Author biography

Musharaf Fayaz is a Indian Author from Srinagar ,J&K, Kashmir and his fathers name is fayaz Anim, he study at dps budgam and is well known for skiing.

CONTENTS

Preface

Warning It is important to stress that there is always a significant danger associated with adventures into the wilderness. Those who wish to follow the adventure hikes in this book should be fully cognizant of those dangers and take appropriate precautions. The accounts are primarily intended for experienced hikers who will exercise informed judgment and caution. The hikes requiring technical expertise and equipment should never be undertaken without proper training and qualifications. Even given all this, the dangers should not be minimized. The accounts are offered with the understanding that readers will proceed entirely at their own risk. In "Precautions" we describe some of the precautions that minimize (but do not eliminate) the dangers and risks.

Acknowledgements

I would like to thank Abeer Bin Javid for helping me in this book.

Ladakh Trip.

Preplanning the trip.Whenever we decide having a trip we float on cloud nine, same was my condition! My family decided to have a trip to Ladakh. Ladakh is a union territory, and is known for its breathtaking mountains, heritage and culture. The beauty of Ladakh just caught my eye. It was so beautiful out there in Ladakh, and my family added more beer and skittles in the trip. As all the others, my family started planning and replanning, and finally it was decided that we will be leaving for the trip on 4thoct, 2021. This made everyone very excited for the trip. As we know, the time flies so finally it was 3rdoct, 2021 the day on which we had to accomplish all our packing. Yes, as usual packing a hectic task! But yet I did accomplish it accurately and on time. Excitement for the trip had wiped me out, but finally it was the last day, and I thought to keep little more patience. Few of my cousins and their family came a night before the trip, as we had to leave early in the morning for it. But I had to complete some work so I didn't take rest instead my accomplished my work. And I'm thankful that my work was completed, Thank god! My family started fitting in all the packages that we had to take along in the cars a night before only, so that there would be no time issues tomorrow. All this was done properly. Now, the excitement was on peak. All were excited! So finally it was 4thoct, 2021!4:00 AM. At the crack of dawn we started getting ready for trip and gathered all the left out necessities. And finally we arranged everything, and we had to leave now. The excitement was floating over the moon now! We finally strike out for trip and I continued to go with my uncle. As a saying goes "No road is long with a good company." So, I too was Happy as Larry with my cousins. We had a whale of time. For the brunch time we had tea and snacks on our way out. We had a lot of mini breaks to relax ourselves in between our road trip. As thankfully I've a big fat family, so we all almost fitted comfortably in almost 6 cars, driven by my father and my uncles. We sailed through the road easily. We crossed Zoji La before and then at 11:00 PM, we reached Kargil War Memorial, and we had a pretty good time there for our relaxing break and we clicked some photographs there as well. Our road trip was endowed with happiness and fun..! As we leaved early in the morning we were dozy that time but because of these fun breaks our doziness was blew away. Though sometimes I used to take a small nap. And on half of the road trip I was with my uncle and then in the half I continued with another uncle. My cousin suffered from motion sickness due to which she looked a little bit under the weather. Two of my uncles also looked a bit off colour. Hallelujah! We reached Singhee palace finally. We freshened up there. So that, a little bit of our somnolence gets diminished for some time. After doing so, we went out for dinner at Hotel Dragon. After we finished having our dinner, we went back to the palace, as it was on a walking distance. We slept then because we were too tired due to a long travel journey. My cousins and I had the same room. So this was all for today. It was a good day overall. And here comes the day, 5th October, 2021. It was pre-planned that we'll be visiting the sites of ladakh on this day. So as usual, we woke up at 8:00AM, had breakfast and got ready for the day. So, we visited the Shanti Stupa and had a lot of fun there, as we know capturing memories by clicking pictures is the important part of every journey, so we did the same. Then we visited the war memorial, where we gathered a lot of information about Indo Pak Wars. That was very interesting though. Next we visited Shey Palace, where a large copper Built of Buddha was made and as per the going, we clicked some pictures there. My uncle was continuously making us Guffaw by cracking jokes.Okay, then we explored a Masjid, which was 700 years old, constructed by Sheikh Ul Alam Hamdani, when he came to Kashmir. We spent pretty good time there, offered Nimaz, and has some snacks. I was not feeling that good, I had body, stomach aches. And even some faced some difficulties while breathing.Then we went to the market, to buy some clothes and other essentials. We went to a restaurant to have sone rolls, and then some shopping again, with my cousin. We had our dinner, and went back to the hotel to take rest, which was much needed especially for me. We were excited for the next day as we had to go to Nubra Valley. Now, it was 6th October, 2021. From the very beginning of the day, almost from 6:00AM I was not feeling well, and that way I couldn't sleep even. Everyone was out for breakfast but my stomach was upset and I didn't have any breakfast. And now, finally at 9:00 AM, we left for Nubra Valley. I decided to travel with my father because as I already mentioned that I was not feeling well. On our way to Nubra Valley, we had a stop at Khardungla Paas, where you can hold on a break for maximum 15 minutes, but my Family stayed there for atleast one hour. There had had a tea break, and some snacks, and as usual some photography was mandatory. Giggles! But this is true that it was only my family not me who were enjoying at that time because of the illness and tiredness I was feeling that time I didn't came out of the car. Woe! In between the car journey my cousin came to drive our car, and suddenly his eye striked at a kind of Grass that was rarely found.He told me to come out of car and collect some of it. I could even now remember that pain when I came out of the car it was like as my hundred bones were cracking at the same time, even more. But by hook or by crook I collected that grass and handed it over to my cousin. I was again not well it was like I could get fainted anytime even I suffered from vomiting. We were still traveling in the car.After some time we reached to a hot spring. While my uncle said me to have a bath to feel refreshed. As everyone was doing the same. That bath is beneficial for the body. I thought I might get well soon by this bath. That was a really good exploration! As we moved towards Changing room now, I suffered from bouts of vomiting that time and I was feeling much tired. Each one of family members except me had a quality time by enjoying the snacks and tea while I was sitting quietly inside the car due to my illness. We travelled for more three to four hours and then finally we reached our resort at Nubra Valley, which was already booked by my uncle, and I appreciate the welcome we had there. That was really a warm welcome. Rooms were allotted to us. We played darts there. Fun! After freshening up we were just wandering around. The dinner we has that day was not that good. We had a bonfire, which was being loved by everyone. We enjoyed a lot there. My family members sung songs, cracked crazy jokes. Ha-ha! Then we went back to our alloted rooms, to take rest as we had to travel more The awaited day, 7th October, 2021. We woke up at 8:30AM, had our breakfast, got ready for the day, and continued our journey to Turtuk. It was a lovely morning and the weather was soothing. We travelled for two to three hours and had a stop on a checkpost, as we were too close to Pakistan border. We enjoyed having some icecreams there. Yummy! Upto 2:00PM we reached Turtuk. There we met an uncle, whose family had stuck in Pakistan when the India Pakistan partition was going on. He had constructed a kind of museum there, where he had stored all the household stuff of ancient times they used to have. Through the he balcony of there house, pakistan border was clearly visible, and inbetween was the no man's land. Few of my cousins wore there traditional dress and photography, which was mandatory though. Then again we travelled for three hours and we reached Yabgo palace Turtuk, which is situated in a Village.Unfortunately the king had gone somewhere, and his daughter explained the full history and everyone was intensely listening to that. After that few members of my family went to buy apricots, which is prominent in Ladakh.As we were in our resort now, One of my cousins also went upstairs, as he had some school exams going on and there was no network in the ground floor. Unluckily, again I found myself not too well that time. I had been sleeping throughout the car journey. And now when we reached I simply hit the sack again, I had body pains, and I didn't even realise what happened when. When my mom came to wake me up for dinner, she found me little bit unwell, I was a kind of fainted that time. My mom called my aunt, she observed that my body was little bit pale. Then she called my uncle, because she thought that my condition was was that good. My uncle checked my saturation and it was in 60's. Firstly we thought that oxyimetre was not working properly but then it was all right. Then the took me to the hospital, where they did my chest X-ray first, and gave me some injections. The tragic thing was that I had been telling my father about this illness for the very beginning of journey.But he thought it might be some common illness that we all suffer from. Now, I was admitted in the army hospital for next two days. The Indian army took good care of mine. That was really appreciated. And that night my mom, dad, and my aunt stayed with me. I was really scared that time, and then doctors informed us that I had been suffering from Pulmonary Edema, which is caused at high elevations. 8th October, 2021. As I was hospitalized already, I woke up at 8:00AM. And for the whole night I didn't feel good, due to the oxygen mask that I had been wearing. I had my breakfast, and my family decided to keep me hospitalized for one more day on precautionary basis. In the evening, my family came to visit me at the hospital. At that day, they had gone to Hunder desert. And they had enjoyed the camel ride as well. Next, we decided to visit Pangong. And then travel back to Leh from there, but the army official told us to take oxygen with ourselves because we had to cross Shangla Pass in between, as we already had that with ourselves so we did the same. Now, we were waiting for tomorrow. 9th October, 2021. "A visit to Pangong." We woke up early at 6:00AM, had our breakfast, got ready for the day. Whole night my cousin, and my father were with me. Now, I travelled with my uncle and aunt in the car, with my oxygen cylinder. Almost at 12:00 we reached Pangong, where woefully my saturation again was in 60's. We clicked some photography as usual, giggles! We had a snack break, and then back to car, Alas! My oxygen was over and done with, and we were yet to cross the Shangla Pass. My uncle not matter what speeded up his car, and thankfully we reached the resort at 5:30. Now, we freshened up and had some snacks. My family went to the market and got some rolls for me. I had my dinner, packed my clothes because tomorrow morning I had to leave for Kashmir. 10th October, 2021. "My last morning in Ladakh." And finally it was the last morning here, thankfully the trip was good overall. I enjoyed my journey to ladakh but due to my sudden illness which caused some halts in my happy journey. But anyway I was thankfully feeling better now. We woke up at 6:00AM, my father dropped us to the airport, me, my mom, and oneof my cousins had decided to travel through Airways now. But rest of my family travelled through road. We finally reached Kashmir, and rest of my family reached till evening, at 9:00PM. "I conclude my ladakh diary, by putting forward my gratitude towards everyone who helped me there.

Hejaz Railway

• Driving time: 4 days • Off-road driving distance: 700 miles • Topo Map: Attached map • Difficulties: 4WD vehicle travel over rough terrain Characteristics On this, the second night of their grand adventure, they had formed the fourwheel-vehicles into a circle beside the rusted remains of an old steam engine, half buried in the sand. Making their camp here under the desert stars, they lit a fire to ward off the chill of the desert night, to focus their conversation and companionship. Talk turned from their tiny and distant homeland of Northern Ireland, to the vast and empty expanses of this Saudi nation. From the great romance of Lawrence of Arabia who wrecked that steam engine, to modern Middle Eastern politics and, inevitably in this day and age, to the wonders of computers, the internet and global communication. They reflected how search engines had allowed a connected people who had dispersed throughout the world to find each other and to communicate again though separated by many thousands of miles - even when that diaspora reached into places as remote as this northwestern corner of the great Arabian desert. Justin listened as his friend described how he had recently used a new search engine to rediscover a great friend from his college days. He resolved to try that when, after this adventure, he returned to the hospital in Riyadh where he was currently employed. But, for the moment, the present adventure was all-consuming and many hundreds of miles of the historic Hejaz Railway would challenge them in the days ahead. For Justin and his friends had set out to follow the route of the Hejaz Railway all the way from Tabuk (28o23.27'N 36o33.55'E) to Medina (24o28.12'N 39o36.65'E), a distance of about 700 miles across one of the most forbidding deserts in the world. The rails and even the sleepers had long ago been borrowed for other purposes, but the raised embankment of gravel and rock along which the railway ran is still extant and can be followed in four-wheel-drive vehicles. The Hejaz Railway was originally built to transport Islamic pilgrims from Damascus to Medina. For untold centuries before, the only method of travel was by camel caravan and the journey would have been arduous and dangerous. The one-way journey alone would have taken about two months. Travel through winter's freezing temperatures and torrential rains, or through the scorching heat of the summer would have been unavoidable. Settlements along the way were sparse and hostile tribes, no doubt, compounded the difficulties. But around the end of the 19th century, the Ottoman empire that dominated the region north of the Arabian peninsula and battled the Arab tribes in an effort to expand into the great desert, raised about eight million pounds from sources such as the Turkish sultan Abdul Hammed, the Khedive of Egypt, and the Shah of Iran to allow construction to begin. That construction posed multifaceted challenges. The engineering problems alone were considerable, since the ground was solid rock in some places, soft and drifting sand in others. Moreover, torrential rain storms would occasionally create flash floods, wiping away bridges and banks and causing the line to collapse. Yet most of the year water was in precious short supply. In addition, the construction crews had to contend with open hostility from local tribesmen and from camel caravan owners whose livelihood was clearly threatened by the railway. Thus most of the construction and maintenance of the line became the responsibility of the Turkish army. Of course, that was part of the Ottoman strategy for the railway would allow the empire to exert a control over the region that was otherwise impossible. The railway was finally opened in 1908 and business boomed in the next few years; the number of pilgrims taking the train mushroomed from 30,000 in 1912 to 300,000 thousand in 1914. In addition, the Turkish government was able to transport a substantial army into the heart of Arabia. But, with the outbreak of the First World War, the pre-existing struggle for dominance of the region between the Ottoman and British Empires, flaired into open aggression. Recognizing the strategic importance of the railway (as well as its vulnerability) the British encouraged the local tribes to cripple that supply line. The most famous instigator of this activity was Thomas E. Lawrence, the legendary Lawrence of Arabia. Many of the trains he sabotaged still lie where they were wrecked. After the war, the Ottoman Empire was dismantled and, though some of the northern sections of the Hejaz Railway continued to function, the long stretch through the Saudi desert melted away leaving only skeletons in the sand. Much, however, still remains to be seen along the deserted route of the railway. The stations, built about 12mi apart, served more as armed watch towers than as stops along the way. Their robust construction meant that they continue to preside over the empty desert.

Adventure Justin and his friends had resolved to follow the route all the way from Tabuk (28o23.27'N 36o33.55'E) in the northwestern desert to the terminus at Medina (24o28.12'N 39o36.65'E), a distance of some 750mi. Their four wheel drive vehicles had been "shipped" to that desert oasis, and there they began their southward journey. The going is rough but not excessively difficult since the rails were removed long ago, and local farmers used the iron sleepers as building supports and fence posts. In the grey, rocky hills outside Tabuk, the expedition first encountered the station at Al Awjariyah, a two-storey fortress built from natural grey stone. From there, following the track along the Wadi Saba for about 8mi brought them to another station, where the track seems to double back on itself. From there it enters a deep gorge and then into a tunnel. The eighth station, Ad Dar Al Hamra (27o20.73'N 37o47.93'E), is situated at the end of a wide, flooded section of the wadi and was built near the ruins of a Turkish fort that they enjoyed exploring. A subsequent station at Al Mutalla has several overturned carriages lying beside it. At Mada'in Saleh (26o48.48'N 37o56.78'E), the station is more extensive with an enormous old engine house, containing several rusting steam locomotives. The station at Al Sawrah, about 72mi south of Al Ula, is one of the most scenic. Situated in a wide, beautiful wadi, the three station buildings are constructed of an attractive yellow stone. Just outside the station one can see the shells of a couple of old pick-up trucks, probably the remains of an attempt to rehabilitate the railway line. Some 21mi south of Al Sawrah twisted iron rails lie buried beside the remains of an engine, sitting bolt upright in the sand despite being some distance from the track itself. An explosion ripped open the metal at the back of the engine and wrecked bogies, blown apart from their carriages, lie nearby. Nothing seems to have changed since 1917. It is not hard to see Lawrence's white robes glinting in the desert sun. Further south is the site of the first mining of the Hejaz Railway at Aba el Naam (25o13.73'N 38o49.45'E). Willie Howard and his wife Janine had journeyed from Lisburn in Northern Ireland to join Justin and two other families on this historic adventure. Thus the talk turned to their native land, to the scarred and battle weary city of Belfast. It was a joy to rekindle their origins but the talk left a shred of sadness as they remembered the lost connections with others that had left to seek a better life in distant lands. Yet there was now new hope of reconnecting. Just as in a byegone age when the advent of railways had allowed families to reconnect, now the internet allowed one to find friends and relatives in the most distant corners of the globe. Epilogue Back in Riyadh, Justin logged onto the Internet and began his search by entering his name into the search engine Google. The number of responses was overwhelming but he soon learned to enter additional words to more narrowly focus the search. Suddenly, there it was - his father's name, his mother's name, even a brief mention of their lives together and of their children. There was even an old photograph of his grandmother as a young girl, standing in a portrait of his great-grandparent's family. All on some webpage he had never seen before on a website somewhere in the United States. In the vernacular of his homeland, Justin was gobsmacked! But he found my name at the bottom of the webpage and the name rang a bell in his distant memory. He vaguely recalled the visit many years ago that he made with his mother and sisters to a village called Magherafelt some 35mi from Belfast where some distant cousins lived. He remembered the boys a few years older than he and the mother who had been such a good friend of his own mother many years before. Indeed his mother had acted as bridesmaid when Wilfred Brennen and Muriel Earls were married in the oncoming shadow of the Second World War. It was strange what the brain was capable of remembering when triggered by a word, a sound or a glimpse. More importantly for the present, Justin found my e-mail address alongside my name and quickly rushed off a message through the new railway of the ether. He also e-mailed his older sister, Caroline Thorpe, who had lived within thirty miles of me for thirty years without knowing either of us was there. So it was that just two days later, I got a second e-mail from Caroline. She, it turned out, was the administrative assistant to the publisher of the Los Angeles Times. About a year earlier, the California Institute of Technology where I work, had held a reception for the publisher of the Los Angeles Times. Caroline had attended that reception. I had attended that reception. We undoubtedly saw each other at the reception. Yet we could have had no idea of each other's presence. It seems really amazing to me that two relatives had come so close without realizing it. Instead it took a casual conversation around a campfire in a strange and remote land plus the magic of the internet for us to make contact and renew the genetic bond. Some technologies make us poorer as human beings; the internet, on the other hand, has an ability to truly enrich us.

Hayna Pichu

• Hiking time: 2 hours • Estimated hiking distance: less than a mile • Elevation gain: 820 feet • Topo Map: Attached map of Huayna Picchu • Permit: Sign in at trailhead Characteristics We had come to this stupendous and storied place to enjoy a shared adventure, perhaps for the last time. This would be a reenactment of a family tradition forged some thirty years earlier when the girls were just a few years old. Adventure was in their souls, perhaps even in their Scotch-Irish genes. Almost forty years before our small nuclear family had left the comfort of a Northern Irish homeland and ventured half way around the world, seeking new spaces in which to grow and prosper. Husband and wife, we had arrived in California with two small daughters, two large suitcases and two hundred dollars; all we had in the world. Since that brave journey there had been joys and sadnesses, triumphs and tragedies. Some the result of happenstance, some caused by the same venturesome spirit that encouraged us to reach for the sky. It had been this way as long as any of us could remember. There had been the long car camping trips throughout the western United States, thousands of miles in a slightly faulty but stylish 65 Mustang to explore every reachable geological oddity or anthropological remnant. We had hiked as far as children's legs could take them, into the Virgin River Narrows, through the Hoh rain forest, up to the glaciers of Mount Rainier and out to a myriad of other places. We had often ventured off-trail to find places others had not seen whether in the rugged and precipitous canyons of the San Gabriel mountains, the wondrous maze of rocks in Joshua Tree National Park, or the canyons of the Colorado plateau, anywhere something new or exciting might be found. Mishaps were, of course, inevitable. In those early days, they rarely meant more than an unexpected dunking or a twisted knee. Sometimes they even meant dangling on the end of a rope for a short time before being rescued. In later life and in different circumstances, there were sometimes more serious consequences. As the eldest daughter she had left home first, traveling across the continent to make her life in an eastern city. She had married an older man, only to discover after two children that their interests and personalities had diverged to the point of rupture. In the heat and trauma of that dissolution, she had become a little derailed. One awful night, Jan.5, 1999, that led to a terrible accident. Driving too fast late at night on icy asphalt, her red 951 Turbo Porsche left the road and smashed, driver side first, into the trees. She was trapped upside down for hours, her lower body crushed among mangled metal. It took more than two hours for the firemen to cut her loose and load her into the helicopter for the short flight to the University of Pennsylvania Hospital. There the doctors diagnosed multiple fractures of the pelvis, two broken femurs, a broken right ankle and numerous lacerations. Orthopedic surgeon Christopher T. Born took on the daunting task of trying to reconstruct the lower part of her body. She was very lucky to have found herself in the hands of this skilled surgeon who performed five operations to reconstruct the pelvis (using five permanent pins), to align the femurs (using a rod through the core of one femur) and pin the ankle together with several permanent screws. She spent two months in the University of Pennsylvania hospital and another month in a rehabilitation hospice in Bryn Mawr. Then many agonizing months with daily physiotherapy in order to walk again. This too was interrupted by a final operation in the fall to remove the rod from the femur. It took patience, persistence and much pain as well as valuable help from her ex-husband, Bill O'Brien. But her innate optimism and irrepressible spirit equipped her for the struggle and within the year she could walk again, albeit slowly and with a limp. Her case was so unusual that Dr. Born published a research paper on it. But she was not finished with the repair and by the summer of 2000 was able to send him a photograph of her rock climbing in Kings Canyon National Park, a picture that he proudly included in the verbal presentation of his paper at a scholarly symposium. But she still limped, was still impaired in her movements so there was still work to be done if she was to live the kind of active life that she had been brought up to and that she wanted for herself and her children. There would be no more horse riding but there could still be great adventure. Now she stood beside me in the midst of the lost city of the Incas. With her sister we had traveled to Peru and flown to the Incan capital of Cuzco. There we paused for several days in that beautiful sky-high city, partly to acclimatize and partly to enjoy the Incan and Spanish colonial history of the place. One guided tour took us to the huge Spanish colonial cathedral of Cuzco, built on the foundations of Incan palaces and richly decorated with imperious, gilded images. During that visit there occurred a moment that augured for something special in our own lives. Standing in the imposing nave of the cathedral, the daunting plumage all around, the cathedral bells began to toll slowly. Moments later the whispers could be heard everywhere and nowhere, "El Papa murio, el Papa murio,...". It was April 2, 2005, and Pope John Paul had just died half a world away. I could not help but be reminded of my own mortality, of the need to relish these special days with my two beloved daughters; ".. never send to know for whom the bell tolls; it tolls for thee (John Donne, 1623)." A couple of days later we caught the early morning train that laboriously switchbacked its way up the mountains surrounding Cuzco and crossed the altiplano before descending again into the deep valley of the Urubamba river.Heading downstream through the ever-deepening gorge we left the dirt roads behind us just northwest of Ollantaytambo, only the railway and the raging Urubamba penetrating the deepening jungle beyond that point. Finally, five hours from Cuzco, the train edged into Agua Caliente (at 13o9.29'S 72o31.51'W), a jumble of vendor stalls, hotels and restaurants squeezed into a strip of jungle between the Urubamba and the towering cliffs. We had come to the land of cloud forest and the mist hung in great clumps over the heights above us. A raft of buses were waiting for the train and we were soon switchbacking our way up the dirt road toward the ridge, 1300ft above the Urubamba, a ridge where the Incas built their magic city of Machu Picchu. We spent the day there, first on a guided tour, and then in our own explorations. The day tours left in mid-afternoon and thereafter we enjoyed the lack of crowds and the improving weather as the mists cleared and the sun began to peek through. It was a glorious afternoon in a magnificent place. Though much of Machu Picchu's history is shrouded in mystery, the most widely held view is that the city was built by the Inca emperor Pachacutec in the mid 1400s and that it served as both a ceremonial and agricultural center. The astronomical alignments of its temples and monuments are very sophisticated and the extensive agricultural terraces may have been used to grow plants adapted to the wet jungle climate rather than the drier Inca heartland. Some think that Machu Picchu's isolation may have led to a decline prior to the Spanish arrival in Peru. What is certain is that it was completely abandoned before it could be discovered by the invaders; Pizzaro marched right past it on his exploration down the Urubamba. This was great good fortune for Machu Picchu was rapidly overgrown and for centuries lay hidden in the jungle, one of the very few Incan cities to escape destruction by the Spaniards. Not until 1911 did the American archaeologist Hiram Bingham uncover its hidden splendors. The city was built on a narrow ridge that lies inside a sharp, 180o bend in the Urubamba river. It is a natural fortress site, easily defended since the 1300ft drop down to the Urubamba is nearly vertical on three sides. On the fourth side, overshadowed by the 10,040ft Machu Picchu mountain, the Inca built a wall, a gate and various guard houses to protect the city. At the other end, the far end of the ridge, a precipitous basaltic column rises like an exclamation mark to a sharp summit, another 1000ft above the city. This awesome pinnacle, known as Huayna Picchu, was sacred to the Incas who managed to built some remarkable structures on its precarious summit. In several places their paths and terraces look down over 2300 vertical feet to the Urubamba. Somehow during the rest of that day and evening, as we relaxed at our hotel in Agua Caliente, a plan to climb Huayna Picchu crystallized in our minds. None of us were quite sure we had the strength after our exhausting travels and the toll that the altitude had taken on our constitutions. When the morning came Kathy, my younger daughter, did not feel well enough for this extracurricular exploit and resolved to spend the morning resting among the Incan ruins. Dana had done nothing like this climb since her accident and so it became an unexpected but welcome test of her long rehabilitation.So it was that in the morning mist we crossed through the lost city to its northwestern end where, at 7875ft, the ridge narrows to a knife-edge. There the Incas built a shrine and guardhouse, a hut (at 13o9.74'S 72o32.80'W) that still serves the same purpose, for those who set off to climb Huayna Picchu today must sign in and sign out when they descend again. It is not quite clear what the authorities would do if someone failed to sign out; drain the Urubamba? We duly signed in and started along the rough trail that first descends about 100ft in order to cross the narrow spine (at 13o9.66'S 72o32.84'W) that connects the main ridge top with Huayna Picchu. The climb up the steep trail toward the summit starts immediately and rapidly steepens; the ancient steps cut into the rock are sorely needed as are the ropes that have been added for modern climbers. We paused often to inhale gulps of thin air. Then on again. Dana climbed easily, exuding a delight in finding final confirmation that she was no longer handicapped; indeed she often had to wait while I caught up. Nearing the summit, the jungle around us merged into Incan walls and soon we were ascending the first steep staircase through those terraces. This led to the first great platform with a fantastic view of Machu Picchu and the land all around us. From this platform the trail proceeded through a short tunnel, emerging beside an "usnu" or holy site with walls built above a 2000ft vertical drop all the way down to the Urubamba. Then more stairs along the edge of that awesome cliff before we arrived at the jumble of giant boulders that adorn the summit. Climbing through and over several of these, overhanging the same huge drop, we finally gained the 8860ft summit of this awesome peak (13o9.44'S 72o32.83'W). As it turned out, Dana had conquered Huayna Picchu with some ease and certainly no limp. Nevertheless the accomplishment symbolized a long and painful struggle, a rehabilitation that had been as much spiritual as physical. It would have been so easy, so comfortable to take refuge in the handicap, to let all those metal pins and rods bear the burden. To make the matter harder, along the way she had to deal with a host of other challenges that would have broken a lesser spirit. So this moment was one of rightful, jubilant celebration. I was and am deeply proud of what my daughter overcame and that pride as well as her joy are etched in the faces of the photographs we took that day. The Incas had carved a soaring condor into the face of the summit boulder. It seemed an appropriate symbol for what she had accomplished.

THE THREE PRESENTS OF D'ARTAGNAN THE ELDER

On the first Monday of the month of April, 1625, the market town of Meung, in which the author of ROMANCE OF THE ROSE was born, appeared to be in as perfect a state of revolution as if the Huguenots had just made a second La Rochelle of it. Many citizens, seeing the women flying toward the High Street, leaving their children crying at the open doors, hastened to don the cuirass, and supporting their somewhat uncertain courage with a musket or a partisan, directed their steps toward the hostelry of the Jolly Miller, before which was gathered, increasing every minute, a compact group, vociferous and full of curiosity.

In those times panics were common, and few days passed without some city or other registering in its archives an event of this kind. There were nobles, who made war against each other; there was the king, who made war against the cardinal; there was Spain, which made war against the king. Then, in addition to these concealed or public, secret or open wars, there were robbers, mendicants, Huguenots, wolves, and scoundrels, who made war upon everybody. The citizens always took up arms readily against thieves, wolves or scoundrels, often against nobles or Huguenots, sometimes against the king, but never against the cardinal or Spain. It resulted, then, from this habit that on the said first Monday of April, 1625, the citizens, on hearing the clamor, and seeing neither the red-and-yellow standard nor the livery of the Duc de Richelieu, rushed toward the hostel of the Jolly Miller. When arrived there, the cause of the hubbub was apparent to all.

A young man--we can sketch his portrait at a dash. Imagine to yourself a Don Quixote of eighteen; a Don Quixote without his corselet, without his coat of mail, without his cuisses; a Don Quixote clothed in a woolen doublet, the blue color of which had faded into a nameless shade between lees of wine and a heavenly azure; face long and brown; high cheek bones, a sign of sagacity; the maxillary muscles enormously developed, an infallible sign by which a Gascon may always be detected, even without his cap--and our young man wore a cap set off with a sort of feather; the eye open and intelligent; the nose hooked, but finely chiseled. Too big for a youth, too small for a grown man, an experienced eye might have taken him for a farmer's son upon a journey had it not been for the long sword which, dangling from a leather baldric, hit against the calves of its owner as he walked, and against the rough side of his steed when he was on horseback.

For our young man had a steed which was the observed of all observers. It was a Bearn pony, from twelve to fourteen years old, yellow in his hide, without a hair in his tail, but not without windgalls on his legs, which, though going with his head lower than his knees, rendering a martingale quite unnecessary, contrived nevertheless to perform his eight leagues a day. Unfortunately, the qualities of this horse were so well concealed under his strange-colored hide and his unaccountable gait, that at a time when everybody was a connoisseur in horseflesh, the appearance of the aforesaid pony at Meung--which place he had entered about a quarter of an hour before, by the gate of Beaugency--produced an unfavorable feeling, which extended to his rider.

And this feeling had been more painfully perceived by young d'Artagnan--for so was the Don Quixote of this second Rosinante named--from his not being able to conceal from himself the ridiculous appearance that such a steed gave him, good horseman as he was. He had sighed deeply, therefore, when accepting the gift of the pony from M. d'Artagnan the elder. He was not ignorant that such a beast was worth at least twenty livres; and the words which had accompanied the present were above all price.

"My son," said the old Gascon gentleman, in that pure Bearn PATOIS of which Henry IV could never rid himself, "this horse was born in the house of your father about thirteen years ago, and has remained in it ever since, which ought to make you love it. Never sell it; allow it to die tranquilly and honorably of old age, and if you make a campaign with it, take as much care of it as you would of an old servant. At court, provided you have ever the honor to go there," continued M. d'Artagnan the elder, "--an honor to which, remember, your ancient nobility gives you the right--sustain worthily your name of gentleman, which has been worthily borne by your ancestors for five hundred years, both for your own sake and the sake of those who belong to you. By the latter I mean your relatives and friends. Endure nothing from anyone except Monsieur the Cardinal and the king. It is by his courage, please observe, by his courage alone, that a gentleman can make his way nowadays. Whoever hesitates for a second perhaps allows the bait to escape which during that exact second fortune held out to him. You are young. You ought to be brave for two reasons: the first is that you are a Gascon, and the second is that you are my son. Never fear quarrels, but seek adventures. I have taught you how to handle a sword; you have thews of iron, a wrist of steel. Fight on all occasions. Fight the more for duels being forbidden, since consequently there is twice as much courage in fighting. I have nothing to give you, my son, but fifteen crowns, my horse, and the counsels you have just heard. Your mother will add to them a recipe for a certain balsam, which she had from a Bohemian and which has the miraculous virtue of curing all wounds that do not reach the heart. Take advantage of all, and live happily and long. I have but one word to add, and that is to propose an example to you--not mine, for I myself have never appeared at court, and have only taken part in religious wars as a volunteer; I speak of Monsieur de Treville, who was formerly my neighbor, and who had the honor to be, as a child, the play-fellow of our king, Louis XIII, whom God preserve! Sometimes their play degenerated into battles, and in these battles the king was not always the stronger. The blows which he received increased greatly his esteem and friendship for Monsieur de Treville. Afterward, Monsieur de Treville fought with others: in his first journey to Paris, five times; from the death of the late king till the young one came of age, without reckoning wars and sieges, seven times; and from that date up to the present day, a hundred times, perhaps! So that in spite of edicts, ordinances, and decrees, there he is, captain of the Musketeers; that is to say, chief of a legion of Caesars, whom the king holds in great esteem and whom the cardinal dreads--he who dreads nothing, as it is said. Still further, Monsieur de Treville gains ten thousand crowns a year; he is therefore a great noble. He began as you begin. Go to him with this letter, and make him your model in order that you may do as he has done."

Upon which M. d'Artagnan the elder girded his own sword round his son, kissed him tenderly on both cheeks, and gave him his benediction.

On leaving the paternal chamber, the young man found his mother, who was waiting for him with the famous recipe of which the counsels we have just repeated would necessitate frequent employment. The adieux were on this side longer and more tender than they had been on the other--not that M. d'Artagnan did not love his son, who was his only offspring, but M. d'Artagnan was a man, and he would have considered it unworthy of a man to give way to his feelings; whereas Mme. d'Artagnan was a woman, and still more, a mother. She wept abundantly; and--let us speak it to the praise of M. d'Artagnan the younger--notwithstanding the efforts he made to remain firm, as a future Musketeer ought, nature prevailed, and he shed many tears, of which he succeeded with great difficulty in concealing the half.

The same day the young man set forward on his journey, furnished with the three paternal gifts, which consisted, as we have said, of fifteen crowns, the horse, and the letter for M. de Treville--the counsels being thrown into the bargain.

With such a VADE MECUM d'Artagnan was morally and physically an exact copy of the hero of Cervantes, to whom we so happily compared him when our duty of an historian placed us under the necessity of sketching his portrait. Don Quixote took windmills for giants, and sheep for armies; d'Artagnan took every smile for an insult, and every look as a provocation--whence it resulted that from Tarbes to Meung his fist was constantly doubled, or his hand on the hilt of his sword; and yet the fist did not descend upon any jaw, nor did the sword issue from its scabbard. It was not that the sight of the wretched pony did not excite numerous smiles on the countenances of passers-by; but as against the side of this pony rattled a sword of respectable length, and as over this sword gleamed an eye rather ferocious than haughty, these passers-by repressed their hilarity, or if hilarity prevailed over prudence, they endeavored to laugh only on one side, like the masks of the ancients. D'Artagnan, then, remained majestic and intact in his susceptibility, till he came to this unlucky city of Meung.

But there, as he was alighting from his horse at the gate of the Jolly Miller, without anyone--host, waiter, or hostler-- coming to hold his stirrup or take his horse, d'Artagnan spied, though an open window on the ground floor, a gentleman, well-made and of good carriage, although of rather a stern countenance, talking with two persons who appeared to listen to him with respect. D'Artagnan fancied quite naturally, according to his custom, that he must be the object of their conversation, and listened. This time d'Artagnan was only in part mistaken; he himself was not in question, but his horse was. The gentleman appeared to be enumerating all his qualities to his auditors; and, as I have said, the auditors seeming to have great deference for the narrator, they every moment burst into fits of laughter. Now, as a half-smile was sufficient to awaken the irascibility of the young man, the effect produced upon him by this vociferous mirth may be easily imagined.

Nevertheless, d'Artagnan was desirous of examining the appearance of this impertinent personage who ridiculed him. He fixed his haughty eye upon the stranger, and perceived a man of from forty to forty-five years of age, with black and piercing eyes, pale complexion, a strongly marked nose, and a black and well-shaped mustache. He was dressed in a doublet and hose of a violet color, with aiguillettes of the same color, without any other ornaments than the customary slashes, through which the shirt appeared. This doublet and hose, though new, were creased, like traveling clothes for a long time packed in a portmanteau. D'Artagnan made all these remarks with the rapidity of a most minute observer, and doubtless from an instinctive feeling that this stranger was destined to have a great influence over his future life.

Now, as at the moment in which d'Artagnan fixed his eyes upon the gentleman in the violet doublet, the gentleman made one of his most knowing and profound remarks respecting the Bearnese pony, his two auditors laughed even louder than before, and he himself, though contrary to his custom, allowed a pale smile (if I may be allowed to use such an expression) to stray over his countenance. This time there could be no doubt; d'Artagnan was really insulted. Full, then, of this conviction, he pulled his cap down over his eyes, and endeavoring to copy some of the court airs he had picked up in Gascony among young traveling nobles, he advanced with one hand on the hilt of his sword and the other resting on his hip. Unfortunately, as he advanced, his anger increased at every step; and instead of the proper and lofty speech he had prepared as a prelude to his challenge, he found nothing at the tip of his tongue but a gross personality, which he accompanied with a furious gesture.

"I say, sir, you sir, who are hiding yourself behind that shutter--yes, you, sir, tell me what you are laughing at, and we will laugh together!"

The gentleman raised his eyes slowly from the nag to his cavalier, as if he required some time to ascertain whether it could be to him that such strange reproaches were addressed; then, when he could not possibly entertain any doubt of the matter, his eyebrows slightly bent, and with an accent of irony and insolence impossible to be described, he replied to d'Artagnan, "I was not speaking to you, sir."

"But I am speaking to you!" replied the young man, additionally exasperated with this mixture of insolence and good manners, of politeness and scorn.

The stranger looked at him again with a slight smile, and retiring from the window, came out of the hostelry with a slow step, and placed himself before the horse, within two paces of d'Artagnan. His quiet manner and the ironical expression of his countenance redoubled the mirth of the persons with whom he had been talking, and who still remained at the window.

D'Artagnan, seeing him approach, drew his sword a foot out of the scabbard.

"This horse is decidedly, or rather has been in his youth, a buttercup," resumed the stranger, continuing the remarks he had begun, and addressing himself to his auditors at the window, without paying the least attention to the exasperation of d'Artagnan, who, however, placed himself between him and them. "It is a color very well known in botany, but till the present time very rare among horses."

"There are people who laugh at the horse that would not dare to laugh at the master," cried the young emulator of the furious Treville.

"I do not often laugh, sir," replied the stranger, "as you may perceive by the expression of my countenance; but nevertheless I retain the privilege of laughing when I please."

"And I," cried d'Artagnan, "will allow no man to laugh when it displeases me!"

"Indeed, sir," continued the stranger, more calm than ever; "well, that is perfectly right!" and turning on his heel, was about to re-enter the hostelry by the front gate, beneath which d'Artagnan on arriving had observed a saddled horse.

But, d'Artagnan was not of a character to allow a man to escape him thus who had the insolence to ridicule him. He drew his sword entirely from the scabbard, and followed him, crying, "Turn, turn, Master Joker, lest I strike you behind!"

"Strike me!" said the other, turning on his heels, and surveying the young man with as much astonishment as contempt. "Why, my good fellow, you must be mad!" Then, in a suppressed tone, as if speaking to himself, "This is annoying," continued he. "What a godsend this would be for his Majesty, who is seeking everywhere for brave fellows to recruit for his Musketeers!"

He had scarcely finished, when d'Artagnan made such a furious lunge at him that if he had not sprung nimbly backward, it is probable he would have jested for the last time. The stranger, then perceiving that the matter went beyond raillery, drew his sword, saluted his adversary, and seriously placed himself on guard. But at the same moment, his two auditors, accompanied by the host, fell upon d'Artagnan with sticks, shovels and tongs. This caused so rapid and complete a diversion from the attack that d'Artagnan's adversary, while the latter turned round to face this shower of blows, sheathed his sword with the same precision, and instead of an actor, which he had nearly been, became a spectator of the fight--a part in which he acquitted himself with his usual impassiveness, muttering, nevertheless, "A plague upon these Gascons! Replace him on his orange horse, and let him begone!"

"Not before I have killed you, poltroon!" cried d'Artagnan, making the best face possible, and never retreating one step before his three assailants, who continued to shower blows upon him.

"Another gasconade!" murmured the gentleman. "By my honor, these Gascons are incorrigible! Keep up the dance, then, since he will have it so. When he is tired, he will perhaps tell us that he has had enough of it."

But the stranger knew not the headstrong personage he had to do with; d'Artagnan was not the man ever to cry for quarter. The fight was therefore prolonged for some seconds; but at length d'Artagnan dropped his sword, which was broken in two pieces by the blow of a stick. Another blow full upon his forehead at the same moment brought him to the ground, covered with blood and almost fainting.

It was at this moment that people came flocking to the scene of action from all sides. The host, fearful of consequences, with the help of his servants carried the wounded man into the kitchen, where some trifling attentions were bestowed upon him.

As to the gentleman, he resumed his place at the window, and surveyed the crowd with a certain impatience, evidently annoyed by their remaining undispersed.

"Well, how is it with this madman?" exclaimed he, turning round as the noise of the door announced the entrance of the host, who came in to inquire if he was unhurt.

"Your excellency is safe and sound?" asked the host.

"Oh, yes! Perfectly safe and sound, my good host; and I wish to know what has become of our young man."

"He is better," said the host, "he fainted quite away."

"Indeed!" said the gentleman.

"But before he fainted, he collected all his strength to challenge you, and to defy you while challenging you."

"Why, this fellow must be the devil in person!" cried the stranger.

"Oh, no, your Excellency, he is not the devil," replied the host, with a grin of contempt; "for during his fainting we rummaged his valise and found nothing but a clean shirt and eleven crowns--which however, did not prevent his saying, as he was fainting, that if such a thing had happened in Paris, you should have cause to repent of it at a later period."

"Then," said the stranger coolly, "he must be some prince in disguise."

"I have told you this, good sir," resumed the host, "in order that you may be on your guard."

"Did he name no one in his passion?"

"Yes; he struck his pocket and said, 'We shall see what Monsieur de Treville will think of this insult offered to his protege.'"

"Monsieur de Treville?" said the stranger, becoming attentive, "he put his hand upon his pocket while pronouncing the name of Monsieur de Treville? Now, my dear host, while your young man was insensible, you did not fail, I am quite sure, to ascertain what that pocket contained. What was there in it?"

"A letter addressed to Monsieur de Treville, captain of the Musketeers."

"Indeed!"

"Exactly as I have the honor to tell your Excellency."

The host, who was not endowed with great perspicacity, did not observe the expression which his words had given to the physiognomy of the stranger. The latter rose from the front of the window, upon the sill of which he had leaned with his elbow, and knitted his brow like a man disquieted.

"The devil!" murmured he, between his teeth. "Can Treville have set this Gascon upon me? He is very young; but a sword thrust is a sword thrust, whatever be the age of him who gives it, and a youth is less to be suspected than an older man," and the stranger fell into a reverie which lasted some minutes. "A weak obstacle is sometimes sufficient to overthrow a great design.

"Host," said he, "could you not contrive to get rid of this frantic boy for me? In conscience, I cannot kill him; and yet," added he, with a coldly menacing expression, "he annoys me. Where is he?"

"In my wife's chamber, on the first flight, where they are dressing his wounds."

"His things and his bag are with him? Has he taken off his doublet?"

"On the contrary, everything is in the kitchen. But if he annoys you, this young fool--"

"To be sure he does. He causes a disturbance in your hostelry, which respectable people cannot put up with. Go; make out my bill and notify my servant."

"What, monsieur, will you leave us so soon?"

"You know that very well, as I gave my order to saddle my horse. Have they not obeyed me?"

"It is done; as your Excellency may have observed, your horse is in the great gateway, ready saddled for your departure."

"That is well; do as I have directed you, then."

"What the devil!" said the host to himself. "Can he be afraid of this boy?" But an imperious glance from the stranger stopped him short; he bowed humbly and retired.

"It is not necessary for Milady* to be seen by this fellow," continued the stranger. "She will soon pass; she is already late. I had better get on horseback, and go and meet her. I should like, however, to know what this letter addressed to Treville contains."

*We are well aware that this term, milady, is only properly used when followed by a family name. But we find it thus in the manuscript, and we do not choose to take upon ourselves to alter it.

And the stranger, muttering to himself, directed his steps toward the kitchen.

In the meantime, the host, who entertained no doubt that it was the presence of the young man that drove the stranger from his hostelry, re-ascended to his wife's chamber, and found d'Artagnan just recovering his senses. Giving him to understand that the police would deal with him pretty severely for having sought a quarrel with a great lord--for in the opinion of the host the stranger could be nothing less than a great lord--he insisted that notwithstanding his weakness d'Artagnan should get up and depart as quickly as possible. D'Artagnan, half stupefied, without his doublet, and with his head bound up in a linen cloth, arose then, and urged by the host, began to descend the stairs; but on arriving at the kitchen, the first thing he saw was his antagonist talking calmly at the step of a heavy carriage, drawn by two large Norman horses.

His interlocutor, whose head appeared through the carriage window, was a woman of from twenty to two-and-twenty years. We have already observed with what rapidity d'Artagnan seized the expression of a countenance. He perceived then, at a glance, that this woman was young and beautiful; and her style of beauty struck him more forcibly from its being totally different from that of the southern countries in which d'Artagnan had hitherto resided. She was pale and fair, with long curls falling in profusion over her shoulders, had large, blue, languishing eyes, rosy lips, and hands of alabaster. She was talking with great animation with the stranger.

"His Eminence, then, orders me--" said the lady.

"To return instantly to England, and to inform him as soon as the duke leaves London."

"And as to my other instructions?" asked the fair traveler.

"They are contained in this box, which you will not open until you are on the other side of the Channel."

"Very well; and you--what will you do?"

"I--I return to Paris."

"What, without chastising this insolent boy?" asked the lady.

The stranger was about to reply; but at the moment he opened his mouth, d'Artagnan, who had heard all, precipitated himself over the threshold of the door.

"This insolent boy chastises others," cried he; "and I hope that this time he whom he ought to chastise will not escape him as before."

"Will not escape him?" replied the stranger, knitting his brow.

"No; before a woman you would dare not fly, I presume?"

"Remember," said Milady, seeing the stranger lay his hand on his sword, "the least delay may ruin everything."

"You are right," cried the gentleman; "begone then, on your part, and I will depart as quickly on mine." And bowing to the lady, he sprang into his saddle, while her coachman applied his whip vigorously to his horses. The two interlocutors thus separated, taking opposite directions, at full gallop.

"Pay him, booby!" cried the stranger to his servant, without checking the speed of his horse; and the man, after throwing two or three silver pieces at the foot of mine host, galloped after his master.

"Base coward! false gentleman!" cried d'Artagnan, springing forward, in his turn, after the servant. But his wound had rendered him too weak to support such an exertion. Scarcely had he gone ten steps when his ears began to tingle, a faintness seized him, a cloud of blood passed over his eyes, and he fell in the middle of the street, crying still, "Coward! coward! coward!"

"He is a coward, indeed," grumbled the host, drawing near to d'Artagnan, and endeavoring by this little flattery to make up matters with the young man, as the heron of the fable did with the snail he had despised the evening before.

"Yes, a base coward," murmured d'Artagnan; "but she-- she was very beautiful."

"What she?" demanded the host.

"Milady," faltered d'Artagnan, and fainted a second time.

"Ah, it's all one," said the host; "I have lost two customers, but this one remains, of whom I am pretty certain for some days to come. There will be eleven crowns gained."

It is to be remembered that eleven crowns was just the sum that remained in d'Artagnan's purse.

The host had reckoned upon eleven days of confinement at a crown a day, but he had reckoned without his guest. On the following morning at five o'clock d'Artagnan arose, and descending to the kitchen without help, asked, among other ingredients the list of which has not come down to us, for some oil, some wine, and some rosemary, and with his mother's recipe in his hand composed a balsam, with which he anointed his numerous wounds, replacing his bandages himself, and positively refusing the assistance of any doctor, d'Artagnan walked about that same evening, and was almost cured by the morrow.

But when the time came to pay for his rosemary, this oil, and the wine, the only expense the master had incurred, as he had preserved a strict abstinence--while on the contrary, the yellow horse, by the account of the hostler at least, had eaten three times as much as a horse of his size could reasonably be supposed to have done--d'Artagnan found nothing in his pocket but his little old velvet purse with the eleven crowns it contained; for as to the letter addressed to M. de Treville, it had disappeared.

The young man commenced his search for the letter with the greatest patience, turning out his pockets of all kinds over and over again, rummaging and rerummaging in his valise, and opening and reopening his purse; but when he found that he had come to the conviction that the letter was not to be found, he flew, for the third time, into such a rage as was near costing him a fresh consumption of wine, oil, and rosemary--for upon seeing this hot-headed youth become exasperated and threaten to destroy everything in the establishment if his letter were not found, the host seized a spit, his wife a broom handle, and the servants the same sticks they had used the day before.

"My letter of recommendation!" cried d'Artagnan, "my letter of recommendation! or, the holy blood, I will spit you all like ortolans!"

Unfortunately, there was one circumstance which created a powerful obstacle to the accomplishment of this threat; which was, as we have related, that his sword had been in his first conflict broken in two, and which he had entirely forgotten. Hence, it resulted when d'Artagnan proceeded to draw his sword in earnest, he found himself purely and simply armed with a stump of a sword about eight or ten inches in length, which the host had carefully placed in the scabbard. As to the rest of the blade, the master had slyly put that on one side to make himself a larding pin.

But this deception would probably not have stopped our fiery young man if the host had not reflected that the reclamation which his guest made was perfectly just.

"But, after all," said he, lowering the point of his spit, "where is this letter?"

"Yes, where is this letter?" cried d'Artagnan. "In the first place, I warn you that that letter is for Monsieur de Treville, and it must be found, or if it is not found, he will know how to find it."

His threat completed the intimidation of the host. After the king and the cardinal, M. de Treville was the man whose name was perhaps most frequently repeated by the military, and even by citizens. There was, to be sure, Father

Joseph, but his name was never pronounced but with a subdued voice, such was the terror inspired by his Gray Eminence, as the cardinal's familiar was called.

Throwing down his spit, and ordering his wife to do the same with her broom handle, and the servants with their sticks, he set the first example of commencing an earnest search for the lost letter.

"Does the letter contain anything valuable?" demanded the host, after a few minutes of useless investigation.

"Zounds! I think it does indeed!" cried the Gascon, who reckoned upon this letter for making his way at court. "It contained my fortune!"

"Bills upon Spain?" asked the disturbed host.

"Bills upon his Majesty's private treasury," answered d'Artagnan, who, reckoning upon entering into the king's service in consequence of this recommendation, believed he could make this somewhat hazardous reply without telling of a falsehood.

"The devil!" cried the host, at his wit's end.

"But it's of no importance," continued d'Artagnan, with natural assurance; "it's of no importance. The money is nothing; that letter was everything. I would rather have lost a thousand pistoles than have lost it." He would not have risked more if he had said twenty thousand; but a certain juvenile modesty restrained him.

A ray of light all at once broke upon the mind of the host as he was giving himself to the devil upon finding nothing.

"That letter is not lost!" cried he.

"What!" cried d'Artagnan.

"No, it has been stolen from you."

"Stolen? By whom?"

"By the gentleman who was here yesterday. He came down into the kitchen, where your doublet was. He remained there some time alone. I would lay a wager he has stolen it."

"Do you think so?" answered d'Artagnan, but little convinced, as he knew better than anyone else how entirely personal the value of this letter was, and saw nothing in it likely to tempt cupidity. The fact was that none of his servants, none of the travelers present, could have gained anything by being possessed of this paper.

"Do you say," resumed d'Artagnan, "that you suspect that impertinent gentleman?"

"I tell you I am sure of it," continued the host. "When I informed him that your lordship was the protege of Monsieur de Treville, and that you even had a letter for that illustrious gentleman, he appeared to be very much disturbed, and asked me where that letter was, and immediately came down into the kitchen, where he knew your doublet was."

"Then that's my thief," replied d'Artagnan. "I will complain to Monsieur de Treville, and Monsieur de Treville will complain to the king." He then drew two crowns majestically from his purse and gave them to the host, who accompanied him, cap in hand, to the gate, and remounted his yellow horse, which bore him without any further accident to the gate of St. Antoine at Paris, where his owner sold him for three crowns, which was a very good price, considering that d'Artagnan had ridden him hard during the last stage. Thus the dealer to whom d'Artagnan sold him for the nine livres did not conceal from the young man that he only gave that enormous sum for him on the account of the originality of his color.

Thus d'Artagnan entered Paris on foot, carrying his little packet under his arm, and walked about till he found an apartment to be let on terms suited to the scantiness of his means. This chamber was a sort of garret, situated in the Rue des Fossoyeurs, near the Luxembourg.

As soon as the earnest money was paid, d'Artagnan took possession of his lodging, and passed the remainder of the day in sewing onto his doublet and hose some ornamental braiding which his mother had taken off an almost-new doublet of the elder M. d'Artagnan, and which she had given her son secretly. Next he went to the Quai de Feraille to have a new blade put to his sword, and then returned toward the Louvre, inquiring of the first Musketeer he met for the situation of the hotel of M. de Treville, which proved to be in the Rue du Vieux-Colombier; that is to say, in the immediate vicinity of the chamber hired by d'Artagnan--a circumstance which appeared to furnish a happy augury for the success of his journey.

After this, satisfied with the way in which he had conducted himself at Meung, without remorse for the past, confident in the present, and full of hope for the future, he retired to bed and slept the sleep of the brave.

This sleep, provincial as it was, brought him to nine o'clock in the morning; at which hour he rose, in order to repair to the residence of M. de Treville, the third personage in the kingdom, in the paternal estimation.

List of Contributors

Musharaf Fayaz (Author)
Abeer BIn Javid (Co- Author)
John Smith (Editor)